Stories of Pirates

Russell Punter

Illustrated by
Christyan Fox

Reading Consultant: Alison Kelly
University of Surrey Roehampton

Contents

Chapter 1

The pesky parrot

It was Charlie Crossbones' first day as a pirate.

He'd spent the last ten years at Pirate School. Now he was ready to set sail for treasure.

He knew how to...

read a treasure map...

unlock a chest...

...and do lots of other piratey things.

4

He even knew how to give a proper pirate's laugh.

What's more, Charlie had been lucky enough to inherit his Grandpa's old pirate ship and all the gear to go with it.

5

But as Charlie looked at his outfit, he realized something was missing. He didn't have a parrot.

A moment later, Charlie spotted just what he needed.

USED PARROT SALE

Get the bird here!

Parrots going cheap!

There were parrots of all shapes and sizes. There was only one problem. They were all too expensive.

As Charlie turned to go, the parrot seller called him back.

"I suppose you could have this one," he said.

Charlie had never seen such a pretty parrot and he was amazed it was so cheap.

Now he had his parrot, Charlie wasted no time in setting off on his hunt for treasure.

9

Out at sea, Charlie spotted a ship called the *Fat Flounder*. He knew it belonged to a rich sailor called Captain Silverside.

Charlie waited until the sailors had gone to lunch. Then he rowed across to the ship and sneaked in through an open window.

Charlie was in luck. He'd climbed into the cabin where the captain kept his treasure.

But he had only just begun to stuff his pockets with gold coins, when disaster struck.

"Sssh!" Charlie hissed at his parrot. But it was too late.

Charlie took one look at
Captain Silverside
and ran.

COME BACK HERE,
YOU SNEAKY THIEF!

The
captain
and his
men chased
Charlie around
the deck six times before the
poor pirate escaped to his boat.

13

As he rowed back to his ship, Charlie turned to his parrot with a face like thunder.

But every time they went to sea, the parrot caused trouble.

Just as Charlie was about to
steal someone's treasure, the
parrot let out a warning cry.

Each time, Charlie only just managed to escape. Soon, he was a nervous wreck. Whenever he tried to get rid of the parrot...

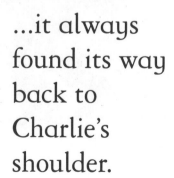

...it always found its way back to Charlie's shoulder.

As Charlie was eating
his supper one evening, he
wondered what he could do.

He had never felt so
miserable. Thanks to that
pesky parrot he was a useless,
practically penniless pirate.

Charlie's long face was making the other customers lose their appetites. The landlord tried to cheer him up.

They were so busy talking, neither of them spotted a thief creeping up to the landlord's cash box.

The thief was just about to swipe all the money, when Charlie's parrot squawked into action.

"What a wonderful bird!" said the landlord. "That thief nearly got away with my cash."

This gave Charlie an idea. Perhaps he could put his parrot to good use after all.

The landlord paid Charlie handsomely for his new burglar alarm...

STOP THIEF!

the parrot enjoyed its new job...

...and Charlie had enough money to buy another bird – a quiet one this time.

Chapter 2

Captain Spike

Macintosh Mullet was a poor fisherman. He lived on tiny Mullet Island with only his daughter, Molly, for company.

One winter, the weather was so bad that Macintosh didn't catch a single fish.

So, Molly put her father's telescope, her best blue vase and a china cat into a wooden chest and set off for the mainland.

Molly had been rowing for ten minutes when she was spotted by Captain Spike and his band of pirates.

In a flash, they dragged her and the chest on board.

The mean captain tried everything to make Molly talk...

Yuck!

...but she wouldn't give him the key.

"Then I'll smash the chest open!" he cried. As he spoke, a thick fog came down around the ship.

"Help!" cried the pirate who was steering. "I can't see!"

"I know these seas," said Molly. "Promise to let me go, and I'll guide you home."

"Hmm... OK," said Spike. "Shark Island, and step on it!"

An hour passed and the fog began to clear a little.

"I'll take over now," said Spike. "I can't have other pirates see you steer my ship, I'd be a laughing stock."

"Can I go then?" asked Molly.
"No!" said Spike, with a sneer.
"You can walk the plank!"

The sneaky captain had broken his promise. Leaving one of his crewmen at the wheel, Spike forced Molly to walk to the end of a plank, into the shark-filled sea below.

But there was no splash... not even a tiny splish. All the pirates heard was a thud!

At that moment, the fog cleared as quickly as it had sprung up.

"This isn't Shark Island!" growled Spike. "She's tricked us. Quick lads! Out of here."

It was too late. Before the pirates could move, the port police jumped on board. Soon, Spike and his men were safely behind bars.

But the port police were still worried about the fog. So they built a lighthouse next to Mullet Island and made Molly the lighthouse keeper.

Chapter 3

The Masked Pirate

Sam Sardine had always wanted to be a sailor.

He was desperate to travel the Seven Seas and do battle with bloodthirsty pirates.

As soon as he was old enough, he joined Captain Winkle's ship as a cabin boy.

But Sam soon found that life on board ship wasn't as exciting as he'd thought.

He spent all day...

mopping the decks...

peeling potatoes...

...and washing the sailors' smelly socks.

Finally, he'd had enough.
He went to the captain and
asked for a proper sailor's job.

Captain Winkle thought Sam
was rather rude. But he decided
to put him to the test.

"All right," he said, "Let's see
you sail the ship into port!"

Sam's chest swelled with pride as he took the wheel.

But steering a ship wasn't as easy as it looked.

Luckily, the ship wasn't too badly damaged. Sam begged for one more chance.

"Very well," said Captain Winkle, at last. "You can guard the ship's treasure."

36

That night,
while the rest
of the sailors
snored in their
bunks,
Sam sat
guard.

But he was
exhausted after his
hard day's
work.
Soon, he
was fast
asleep
as well.

zzz..!

Hours later, Sam was woken from his dreams by a wicked laugh.

He rushed up on deck, to see the dreaded Masked Pirate sailing off with Captain Winkle's treasure.

Sam felt terrible. What would the captain say? He didn't have to wait long to find out.

When Captain Winkle had calmed down, he offered a reward to whoever could track down the thief or his treasure.

But, as the pirate always wore a mask, no one knew what he looked like.

Suddenly, Sam had an idea.

I'll find the pirate *and* your treasure.

Captain Winkle didn't have much confidence in his cabin boy, but no one else had a plan.

That evening, Sam went to the Spyglass Inn, where the local pirates spent the night.

At breakfast next morning, Sam said in a loud voice, "I heard the Masked Pirate talking in his sleep last night."

One particular pirate sitting in a corner began to look worried. Sam's plan was working.

"Now I know where the treasure is, I'm going to get it for myself!" Sam went on.

Hearing this, the pirate rushed out of the inn. Sam followed close behind.

The pirate jumped into a boat and rowed to an island just off the coast.

Sam ran to Captain Winkle.

When they arrived
on the island, they
found the pirate
hurriedly
digging up
a treasure
chest.

45

The captain recognized it at once. It was *his* treasure chest. Taking a flying leap, he landed on the pirate.

"Take my ship and fetch help, Sam my boy!" he roared.

"You trust me to sail?" cried Sam. "Aye aye, Captain!"

There are lots more great stories for you to read:

Usborne Young Reading: Series One
Aladdin and his Magical Lamp
Animal Legends
Stories of Dragons
Stories of Giants
Stories of Gnomes & Goblins
Stories of Magical Animals
Stories of Princes & Princesses
Stories of Witches
The Burglar's Breakfast
The Dinosaurs Next Door
The Monster Gang
Wizards

Usborne Young Reading: Series Two
A Christmas Carol
Aesop's Fables
Gulliver's Travels
Jason & The Golden Fleece
Robinson Crusoe
The Adventures of King Arthur
The Amazing Adventures of Hercules
The Amazing Adventures of Ulysses
The Clumsy Crocodile
The Fairground Ghost
The Incredible Present
Treasure Island

Series editor:
Lesley Sims

CLANK!
CLANK!

First published in 2003 by Usborne Publishing Ltd., Usborne House,
83-85 Saffron Hill, London EC1N 8RT, England. www.usborne.com
Copyright © 2003 Usborne Publishing Ltd.